SPLATypus

BY Sudipta Bardhan-Quallen

ILLUSTRATED BY Jackie Urbanovic

two lions

Published by Two Lions, New York
www.apub.com

Amazon, the Amazon logo, and Two Lions are trademarks of Amazon.com, Inc.,
or its affiliates.

ISBN-13: 9781503939202 (hardcover)
ISBN-10: 1503939200 (hardcover)
ISBN-13: 9781503939219 (paperback)
ISBN-10: 1503939219 (paperback)

Book design by Abby Dening
Printed in China
First edition
10 9 8 7 6 5 4 3 2 1

To Kami, who never lets me give up,
no matter how many times I SPLAT!–*S.B.Q.*

For everyone who has learned
from their mistakes, me included!–*J.U.*

Lonely day
on the bay
Platypus just wants to play.

"Where to go?"
asks Platypus.

Kangaroos
jump-a-roo,
so he hollers, "I'll jump too!"

Here comes Platypus . . .

SKIPPING,

HOPPING,

DIPPING,

DROPPING.

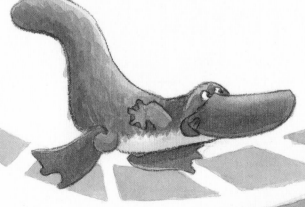

LOOK OUT,

SPLATypus!

Far too jumpy,
far too bumpy,
this is not for Platypus.

"Not to be,
but wait and see!
I will find
the place for me!"

Dingoes chase
and run with grace.
Platypus says, "I'll go race!"

STUMBLE, BUMBLE,

TAKE A TUMBLE,

DIZZY, SPINNY

SPLATypus!

That went wrong.
Jumps up strong!
"Soon I'll find
where I belong!"

Possums bound
above the ground.
Platypus will leap around.

HOBBLE,
BOBBLE,
WIGGLE,
WOBBLE.

Says good-bye
with a sigh.
"I'll go somewhere
else and try."

Fruit bats fly across the sky. Platypus says, "I'll soar high!"

FLIPPING,

FLOPPING,

FLAPPING,

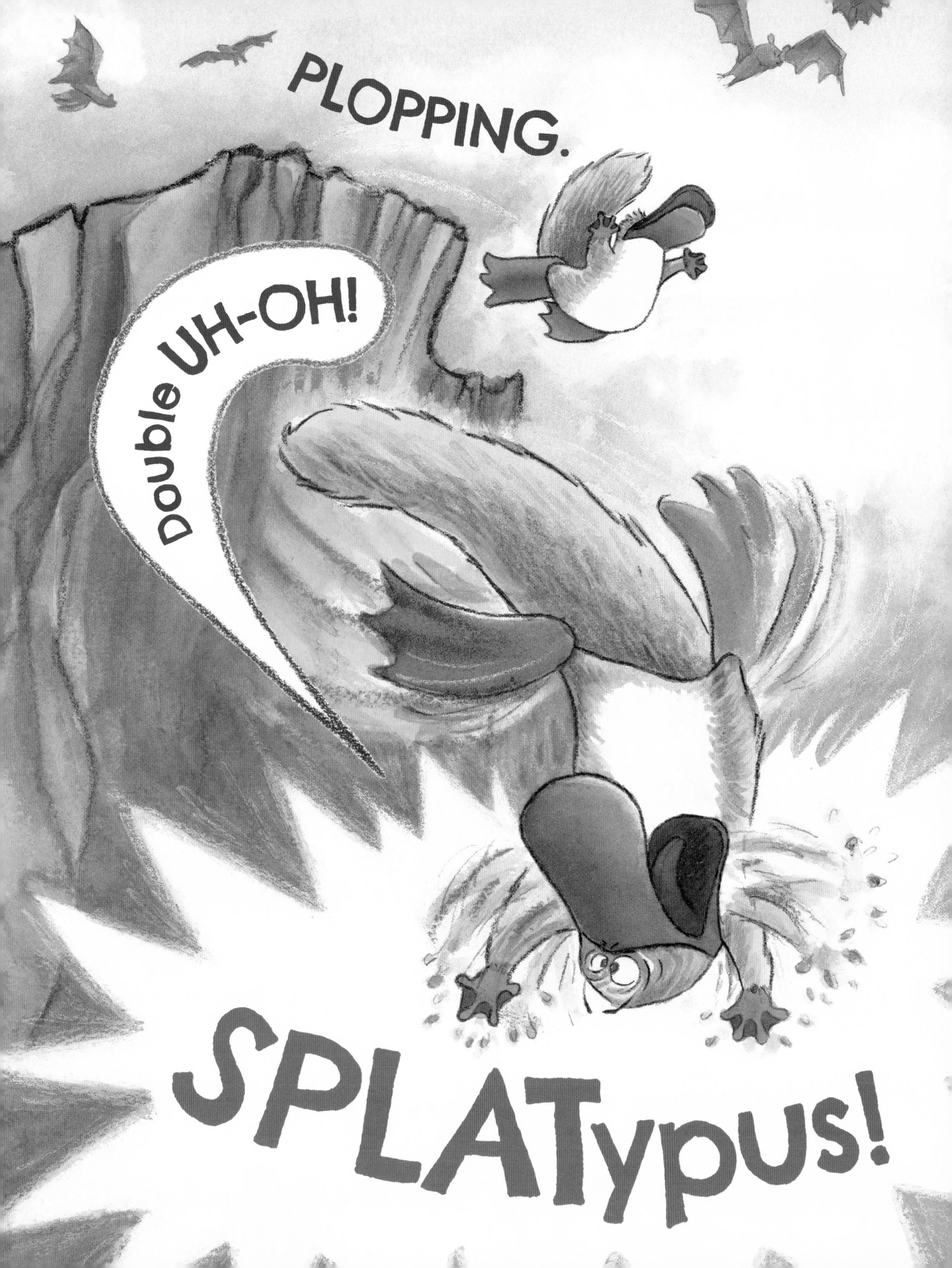
PLOPPING.
Double UH-OH!
SPLATypus!

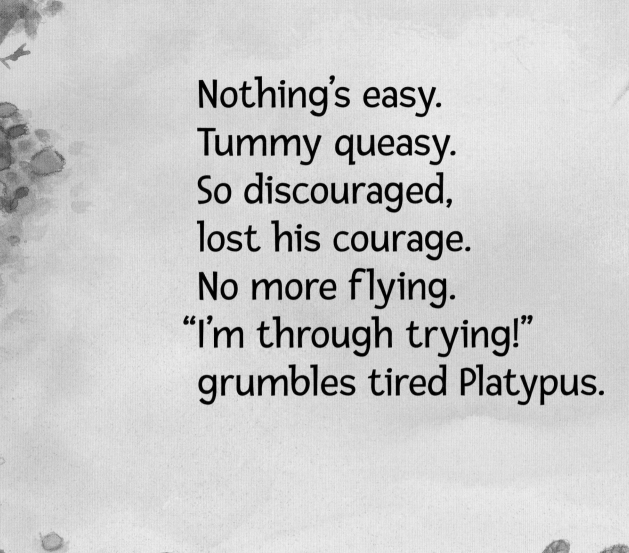

Nothing's easy.
Tummy queasy.
So discouraged,
lost his courage.
No more flying.
"I'm through trying!"
grumbles tired Platypus.

Sun descends.
Daylight ends.
Still no place and
still no friends.

Poor, poor
Platypus.

Morning sun,
the day's begun.
Platypus whines, "Won't be fun."

But then he spies
some swans swim by.

Soon penguins cry
a soggy "Hi!"

His reply,
though feeling shy,
"Maybe I'll give
one last try...."

TEETER-TOTTER

to the water,
jump in with a

SPLITTER-SPLOTTER.

KER-SPLOOSH, KER-SPLASH, SPLATYpus!

Water wiggling,
all are giggling.

DIVING, DIPPING, SLIDING, SLIPPING.

Wait a minute,
swimming in it!

Looks around,
at last he's found
the perfect place for **SPLATypus.**